Baggy Brown started out very well indeed. He was made with 999 others just like himself as a Special Limited Edition costing £499.99 each.

In his ear was a golden button in the shape of a crown. Do you know why that was?

Because Baggy Brown was made to celebrate the first birthday of her Royal Highness Princess Sophinyiniannia, first-born and daughter to the King and Queen of Thingland.

First published in 2007
This paperback edition first published in 2008
by Hodder Children's Books.

Copyright © Mick Inkpen 2007

Hodder Children's Books
338 Euston Road, London, NW1 3BH

Hodder Children's Books Australia
Level 17/207 Kent Street, Sydney, NSW 2000

The right of Mick Inkpen to be identified as the author
and illustrator of this Work has been asserted by him in
accordance with the Copyright, Designs and Patents Act 1988.

A catalogue record of this book is
available from the British Library.

ISBN: 978 0 340 93231 5
10 9 8 7 6 5 4 3 2

Printed in China

Hodder Children's Books is a
division of Hachette Children's Books.
An Hachette Livre UK Company
www.hachettelivre.co.uk

Baggy Brown
Mick Inkpen

Hodder
Children's
Books

A division of Hachette Children's Books

Princess Sophinyiniannia, (Sophie for short), also started out well, as you can imagine.

To give you some idea, this is just the top of the pile of cuddly toys that arrived for her the very day she was born.

But do you know, not one of them could stop her crying. Week after week her little howls rang right royally throughout the palace.

In fact her cries were so upsetting that the King and Queen had to pull their crowns over their ears!

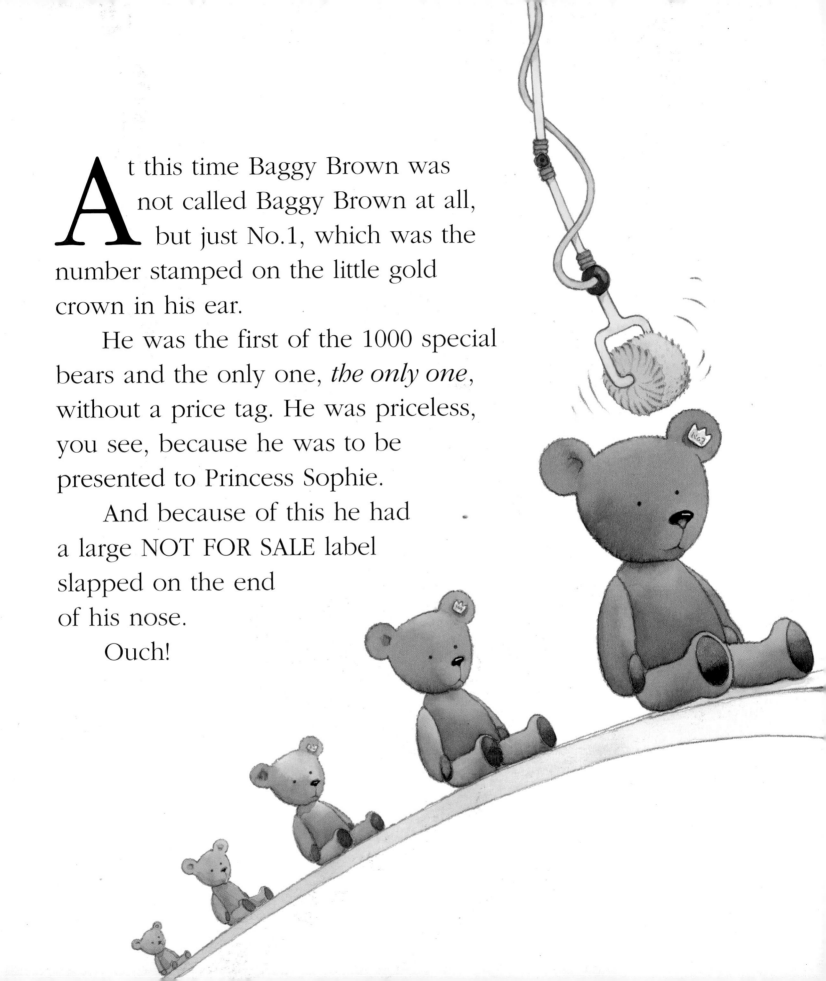

At this time Baggy Brown was not called Baggy Brown at all, but just No.1, which was the number stamped on the little gold crown in his ear.

He was the first of the 1000 special bears and the only one, *the only one*, without a price tag. He was priceless, you see, because he was to be presented to Princess Sophie.

And because of this he had a large NOT FOR SALE label slapped on the end of his nose.

Ouch!

It was such a shock that Baggy Brown did not line himself up properly when the big grabbler came round. It missed him completely!

While all the other bears were grabbled and whizzed away, No.1 continued along the conveyor belt and fell straight off the end.

Down he fell, down, down, and back into the very innards of the big red teddy bear machine at Better Bears Ltd.

He was grubbed and fluffed
and plumped and scrodged
and frizzled and squidged
and pummelled and hooshed
and hooshed
and hooshed again!
And when it had finished with
him, the big red teddy bear machine
spat him out onto the factory floor,
where a passing factory worker
called Jack trod on him.

ow Jack wasn't to know
that Baggy Brown was a
priceless bear. He certainly
didn't look like one. So he picked
him up and took him home for his
young son, Alfie.

Alfie loved Baggy Brown from
the moment he saw him. He loved
his lopsided face and his soft, saggy
body. He loved, too, the strange
gold button under Baggy Brown's
squashed ear, even though he could
make no sense of the name on it.

'No. . . 1?' read Alfie slowly.
'No one is a silly name for
a bear.' And he began to
think of a proper name.

For three days Alfie carried Baggy Brown everywhere with him. But on the fourth day he hid him, and I will tell you why.

On that day the television news finished with a story about a missing royal bear. 'Number One, first in a long line of bears, is missing!' said the reporter. He was holding up No.2 bear.

'Number One! No.1! That's you Baggy Brown!' said Alfie.

And that is why, almost as soon as Baggy Brown got his real name, he was being stuffed head first into one of Jack's smelly old wellies.

That night Alfie couldn't sleep.
He crept downstairs and
rescued Baggy Brown from
the stair cupboard. Silently he opened
the front door and stepped out into
the cool night.

Alfie knew his way through all
the narrow alleyways that led down
to the banks of The Great River.
He knew too all the watery places
where the coal barges slopped
against the wharves. And he knew
exactly which boat would head off
into the city before first light.

It was into this that he
jumped, curled himself into
a ball around Baggy Brown,
and fell asleep.

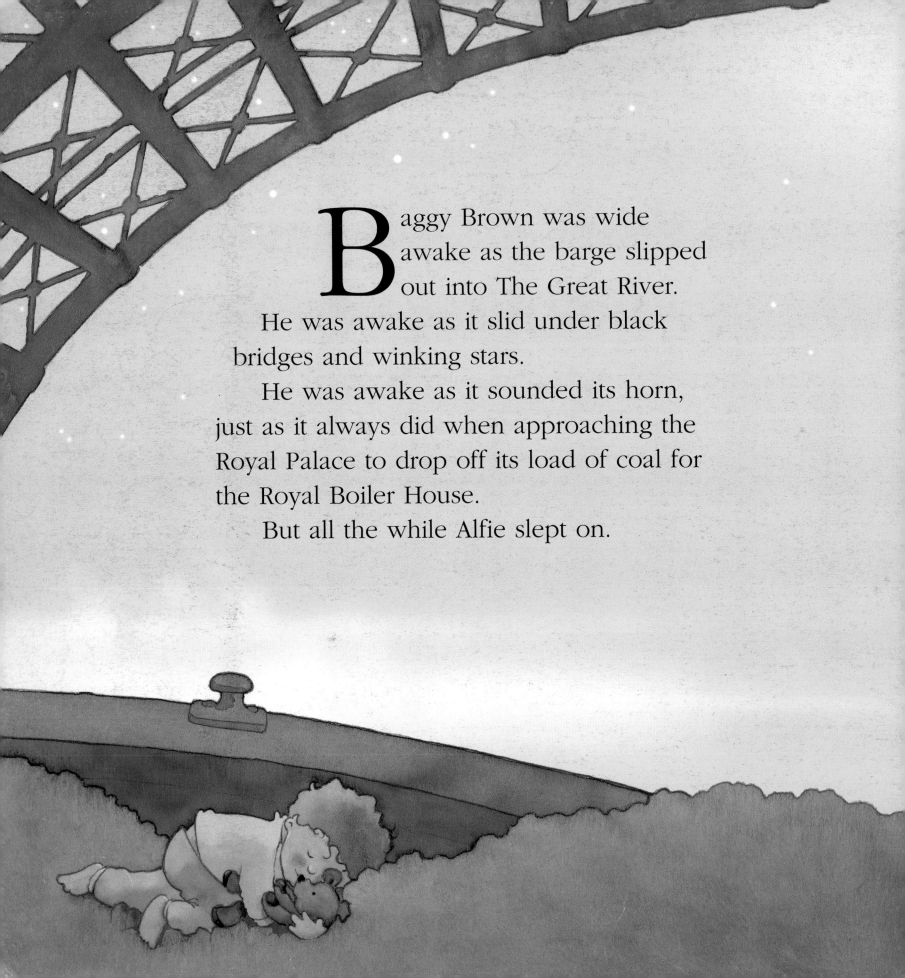

Baggy Brown was wide
awake as the barge slipped
out into The Great River.

He was awake as it slid under black
bridges and winking stars.

He was awake as it sounded its horn,
just as it always did when approaching the
Royal Palace to drop off its load of coal for
the Royal Boiler House.

But all the while Alfie slept on.

Which is how he was
found by the Royal Stoker.
The Stoker, who did not
have a clue what to do with the
grubby little boy and his grubby little
bear, summoned a Royal Footman.

'This belongs to the Princess!'
said Alfie holding up Baggy Brown.

The Stoker and the Footman
burst into laughter.

'I don't think so, son,' said
the Stoker.

'Don't be ridiculous!'
said the Footman. 'And
take that disgusting
object away!'

B ut Alfie refused to budge. 'It does!' he said. 'It belongs to the Princess!' So the Footman sent for one of the Ladies in Waiting.

Lady Jane Farque-Hurrah was undaunted by the smell of old welly rising from Baggy Brown. And having five children of her own, she knew exactly when a child was telling the truth.

She examined Baggy Brown closely. As she lifted his coal black ear there was a bright glint of gold.

'Aha!' she said, and read aloud, 'No.1!'

'His name is Baggy Brown,' said Alfie.

After a quick clean up with Lady Jane Farque-Hurrah's hanky, Alfie was led through the Palace to the Royal Nursery where Princess Sophie was howling as usual.

Sophie looked at Alfie.
She looked at Baggy Brown.
She stopped crying!
And for the first time in fifty-three weeks the Royal Palace was quiet.

Sadly Alfie pushed Baggy Brown through the bars of the Royal Cot and was led away. But at this moment Sophie started to howl even louder than before!

'Alfie,' whispered Lady Jane, 'it's not Baggy Brown that Sophie wants. . .

. . . it's you!'

S o that sealed it. Alfie was allowed to keep Baggy Brown, which of course meant that Baggy Brown was allowed to keep Alfie.

And what about Sophie?
Well the following week a parcel arrived for Alfie. In it was a silver phone with just one golden button. From that day on, whenever he liked, Alfie could call for the Royal Barge to take him and his friends up The Great River to the Royal Palace to visit Sophie.
This is them in the treehouse that the King had built in the Palace Garden when Sophie was five and Alfie was nine.

And if I had longer to tell you what happened, I would tell you that Sophie loved Alfie and his baggy brown bear for the rest of her life, and married him just after her 21st birthday.

I would tell you that Alfie's father, Jack, became the proud owner of Better Bears Ltd, but his proudest day was the day he learned that his grandson, future King of Thingland, was to be named after him.

I would tell you that on the day His Royal Highness Prince Jack was born, 10,000 bears rolled off the conveyor belt at Better Bears Ltd. . .

. . . and I would tell you that
none of them was loved as
much as Baggy Brown.